A LITTLE
PEACEFUL
SPOT

Written & Illustrated
by Diane Alber

To my children, Ryan and Anna,

Always remember, your PEACEFUL SPOT is always there, you just need to find it!

This book belongs to:

_____

_____

_____

Hi! I'm a PEACEFUL SPOT!

Your PEACEFUL SPOT helps you
feel RELAXED and CALM.

And today I'm going to show YOU how to get

to your PEACEFUL SPOT!

TA-DA! Here it is! Isn't it beautiful?

Because you are CALM and RELAXED right now, it's really easy to SPOT.

But when a BIG SPOT of EMOTION shows up, it can become OVERWHELMING. And then it can be hard to see this CALM, PEACEFUL SPOT.

That's why it's important to look
for your PEACEFUL SPOT as soon as one of these SPOTS of
EMOTION starts to get too BIG!

But first you need to identify what SPOT of
EMOTION shows up...

Is it your ANGRY SPOT?

Are you feeling FRUSTRATED because you can't find something?
Or ANNOYED because you tried to do something and it didn't
turn out like you expected?

Or your ANXIETY SPOT?

Are you feeling WORRIED about trying something new? Or SCARED that you won't pass your test?

Or is it your SADNESS SPOT?

Are you feeling LONELY because no one will play with you?
Or DISAPPOINTED because you dropped your
delicious popsicle?

Each EMOTION can be managed in a different way. That is why it is important to identify which one you are feeling.

Nervous   Worried   Scared

Disappointed   Lonely   Loss

Annoyed   Hurt   Frustrated

Once you have identified the SPOT of EMOTION, it makes it easier to guide it to your PEACEFUL SPOT.

If you are having a hard time figuring out which SPOT of EMOTION it is, it can help if you write or draw how you are feeling.

Now it's time to turn that SPOT of EMOTION into a PEACEFUL SPOT. Sometimes it helps to fill your PEACEFUL SPOT with a lot of amazing PEACEFUL THINGS.

Let's look at some times when you were PEACEFUL! Let's add those things to your PEACEFUL SPOT!

Get some crayons and paper for some PEACEFUL COLORING!

Or, find some PEACEFUL MUSIC.

How about some BOOKS for PEACEFUL READING and WRITING?

Or some PEACEFUL PICTURES for MEDITATION?

Let's add a chart for CALM breathing, too!

SPOT PATTERN BREATHING

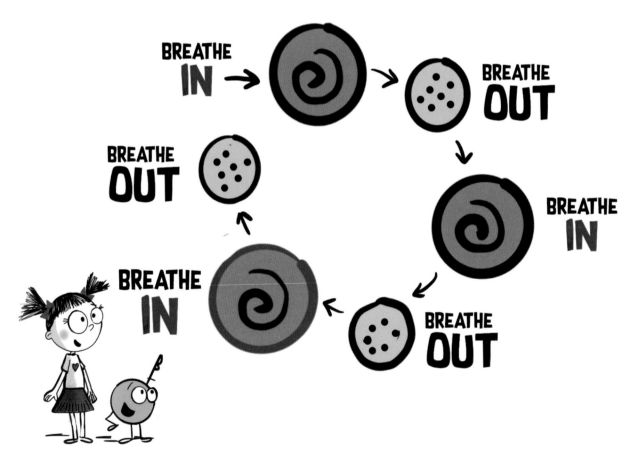

Imagine a pattern of several green SPOTS.
Breathe IN with the swirls and OUT with the dots.
My emotions are now in this peaceful place,
I will be CALM when I leave this space.

Here are some other BREATHING tricks
you can do, too. Each saying is for a different EMOTION!

Count the SPOTS from one to four.
Tap, tap, tap and tap once more.
Now fill your lungs
with peaceful air,
and coat your spots
with love and care.

From the tip of my finger to the middle of my palm,
I can do this! I can be calm!
This worry grew too big and cannot stay,
take a deep breath and blow it away!

Circle the SPOTS in the middle of your palm,
count the swirls down to CALM.
Around and around, and around twice more.
One, then two, then three, then four.
Each time you trace around the SPOTS,
take a deep breath to CALM your thoughts.

Oh wow! It's working already!
Look how CALM he looks!
And I love the big, cozy chair, too!

Okay, I think I've given you enough tools to help you find your PEACEFUL SPOT!

I'll be looking forward to seeing you soon!

Imagine a pattern of several green SPOTS.

Breathe IN with the swirls and OUT with the dots.

My emotions are now in this peaceful place,

I will be CALM when I leave this space.

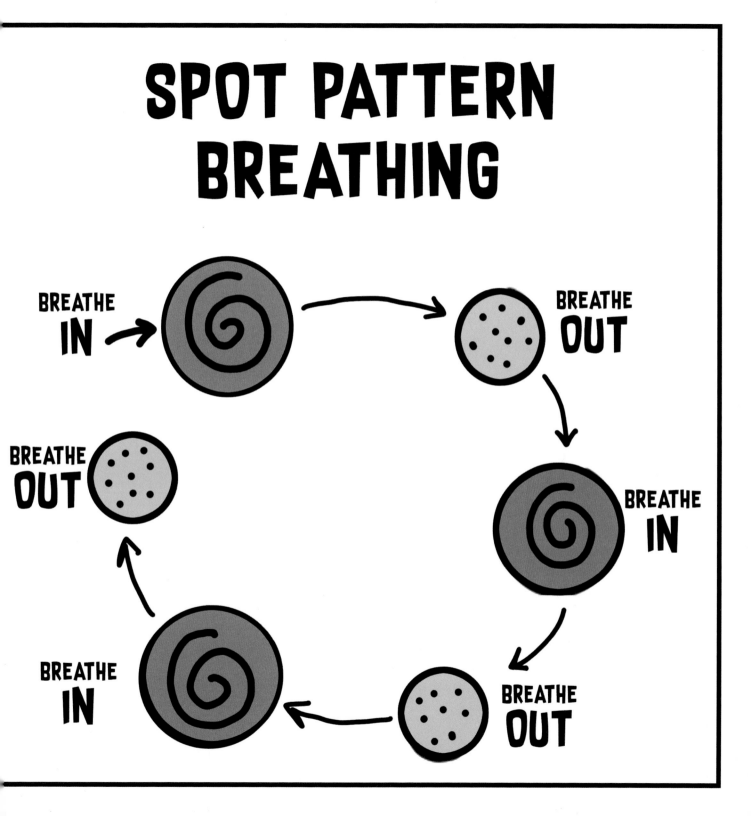

SPOT YOUR FEELING

Nervous

Worried

Scared

Disappointed

Lonely

Loss

Annoyed

Hurt

Frustrated

BREATHING TRICKS

Count the SPOTS from one to four.
Tap, tap, tap and tap once more.
Now fill your lungs
with peaceful air,
and coat your spots
with love and care.

From the tip of my finger to the middle of my palm,
I can do this! I can be calm!
This worry grew too big and cannot stay,
take a deep breath and blow it away!

Circle the SPOTS in the middle of your palm,
count the swirls down to CALM.
Around and around, and around twice more.
One, then two, then three, then four.
Each time you trace around the SPOTS,
take a deep breath to CALM your thoughts.